BRATZ
Clued In!

Behind-the-Scenes
Secrets
by Leslie Goldman

Grosset & Dunlap

D0190545

GROSSET & DUNLAP
Published by the Penguin Group
Penguin Group (USA) Inc., 375 Hudson Street, New York, New York 10014, U.S.A.
Penguin Group (Canada), 10 Alcorn Avenue, Toronto, Ontario, Canada M4V 3B2
(a division of Pearson Penguin Canada Inc.)
Penguin Books Ltd, 80 Strand, London WC2R 0RL, England
Penguin Ireland, 25 St Stephen's Green, Dublin 2, Ireland
(a division of Penguin Books Ltd)
Penguin Group (Australia), 250 Camberwell Road, Camberwell,
Victoria 3124, Australia (a division of Pearson Australia Group Pty Ltd)
Penguin Books India Pvt Ltd, 11 Community Centre, Panchsheel Park,
New Delhi – 110 017, India
Penguin Group (NZ), Cnr Airborne and Rosedale Roads, Albany,
Auckland 1310, New Zealand (a division of Pearson New Zealand Ltd)
Penguin Books (South Africa) (Pty) Ltd, 24 Sturdee Avenue,
Rosebank, Johannesburg 2196, South Africa

Penguin Books Ltd, Registered Offices:
80 Strand, London WC2R 0RL, England

 www.bratzpack.com

Used under license by Penguin Young Readers Group. Published in 2005 by Grosset & Dunlap, a division of Penguin Young Readers Group, 345 Hudson Street, New York, New York 10014. GROSSET & DUNLAP is a trademark of Penguin Group (USA) Inc. Printed in the U.S.A

Library of Congress Cataloging-in-Publication Data

Goldman, Leslie.
  Behind-the-scenes secrets / by Leslie Goldman.
    p. cm.— (Clued in! ; 1)
  "Bratz."
  Summary: The girls offer to help out backstage at a fashion-show fundraiser, but when strange accidents threaten to sabotage the event, they have to save the show.
  ISBN 0-448-43963-8 (pbk.)
  [1. Fashion shows—Fiction. 2. Models (Persons)—Fiction. 3. Friendship—Fiction. 4. Mystery and detective stories.] I.Title. II. Series.
  PZ7.G5686Beh 2005
  [Fic]—dc22

2005003387

10 9 8 7 6 5 4 3 2 1

BRATZ Clued In!

Behind-the-Scenes
Secrets

Chapter 1

Cloe, Yasmin, and Sasha were all in art class, wondering where Jade could be.

"The late bell rang ten minutes ago," said Cloe.

"I'm sure she'll show up soon," Sasha said. "She's so into this project."

"I can see why," said Yasmin, taking a few steps back from it so she could get a fresh look. "This mural is so awesome."

Last Monday their art teacher, Mr. Del Rio, had asked them to get into groups of four to paint murals. This was the perfect assignment for Yasmin, Cloe, Jade, and Sasha. Not only were they all in that class, but they were also the very best of friends. No surprise, since they had so much in common. Caring about one another was high on that list. A passion for fashion followed soon after.

They'd been working all week on the design for the mural. It was going to be a mega-huge runway. They were in the middle of adding life-size portraits of themselves strutting down the catwalk.

The Yasmin in the mural was cute and thoughtful, just like the real Yasmin. She wore a pair of Ysabel Florente jeans, which made sense since Ysabel Florente was her favorite designer.

The jeans rested at her hips and flared out at her ankles. She had on chunky red heels with sparkles and a bright pink tank with a soft, fuzzy, light pink cardigan over it. Her hair was pulled back from her face with a cute silver headband.

They'd painted Cloe's golden-blond hair perfectly. It was swept to one side and resting on her shoulder. Her image looked fabulous in a purple mini-dress with a long red stripe going down one side, and high black boots. Her painted face wore an expression of warmth, friendliness, and determination, just like the real Cloe.

Of the four best friends, Sasha was the ever-so-practical go-getter. She aspired to be a record producer with her own fashion line when she grew up, and everyone knew she'd definitely succeed. In her mural image she looked the part. She'd painted herself in sleek black pants and an orange, blue, and lime green sheer top. Her hair was swept up in a bun with wispy strands hanging down around her face. On her feet she'd painted on a pair of bright blue, sparkly mules.

It was all so fabulous. The girls couldn't imagine getting anything less than an A-plus for their work. They were only missing a couple of things.

The first was an image of Jade. She loved fashion so much, she couldn't decide on an outfit to wear for her portrait, so they had agreed to paint her last. And the second thing they were missing was the real live Jade, in the flesh.

"Where is she?" asked Cloe again,

impatiently. "Kool Kat is never *this* late for class."

Kool Kat was Jade's nickname. She was as cool as could be and loved cats of all colors, shapes, and sizes.

Just then she walked into the room, totally out of breath. "You guys—I have the most rockin' news."

"You finally figured out what to wear in your painting?" asked Sasha. "I hope so because this is all due soon."

"No," said Jade. "This is way more exciting

than our mural. Guess who's coming to town to do a fashion show?" She asked the question and then answered before anyone could even guess. "Ysabel Florente!"

"No way!" Yasmin gasped. "Ysabel Florente, the world-famous designer?"

"Yup," said Jade.

"Ysabel Florente who's totally Italian posh? Ysabel Florente who's the top of the top? Ysabel Florente, the designer whose career we've been following, like, forever?" asked Yasmin.

"Yes, yes, and absolutely yes!" said Jade.

"I can't believe it!" said Cloe.

All the girls were super-excited. They jumped up and down and gave one another high-fives.

"Ysabel's clothes are the coolest," said Sasha.

"They're so flattering and they go well with any occasion."

"I've got two words for you," said Jade. "Fashion Sense. Before becoming a designer, Ysabel ruled the runway in Europe. She was the most famous model of her day."

"No kidding," Cloe added. "And I'm so totally honored that her show is going to be held in our hometown."

Yasmin was the most excited. "Ysabel Florente designs my favorite jeans," she said in an excited voice. "And even better, Ysabel is a big environmentalist and an animal-rights activist. I think I read about this show in last month's issue of *Fashion Forward*. Is this the one she's doing in order to raise money for an animal shelter?"

"It sure is," said Jade. "I love that we're going to get to help out at the show *and* help all those poor homeless cats. And I haven't even told you the best part! The fashion show is going to be in the gym, here at Stiles High."

"No!" said the others.

"Yes," said Jade. "And I volunteered us to help out backstage. I knew you guys would be into it. We're going to meet Ysabel Florente and all of her models."

Yasmin beamed. When she'd read about the show, Ysabel was still trying to decide where to hold it. "This is the best news I've gotten since Unique Boutique put all their tank tops on sale!"

"No kidding," Jade said. "And this'll be way better than that, I promise."

"What do you mean?" wondered Cloe.

"Those tanks totally went out of style like the minute we left the store," said Jade.

Chapter 2

No way could the girls focus on the mural anymore. Instead they did a victory dance, waving their arms over their heads, shaking their hips, and totally getting down to an imaginary beat.

"You're still in my class," Mr. Del Rio reminded them. "You should at least pretend you're working on the mural project."

"We are," Cloe insisted. "This is all part of the creative process."

As soon as class let out, Sasha sprang into action. "We've got to make sure everything runs smoothly. We'll show Ysabel the best time. So what are our assignments?"

"Beats me," said Jade. She handed over the list of tasks. "I haven't even read this yet."

Sasha read the list and then pulled out her own notebook. Of all the girls, she was known as the one who got things in order. "Okay, this is a no-brainer. Jade, you can help out with wardrobe, and I'm going to work with the sound people."

"Good idea," said Yasmin. Everyone knew that Sasha planned on going into the music business when she graduated from school, so it made complete sense that she'd want to manage all the technical aspects.

"And Yasmin, since Ysabel designs your favorite jeans, and you guys obviously have the most in common, you can be her personal assistant for the days leading up to the show," said Sasha.

Yasmin jumped up and down. "Thank you, thank you, thank you." Yasmin couldn't wait to meet Ysabel. She knew they were going to bond. It wasn't just her designs, but her whole being that Yasmin loved. Ysabel drove a hybrid car to help eliminate pollution, and whenever Ysabel threw a fashion show, she requested that the concession stands go vegetarian.

The girls were still talking about the show when Cameron and Dylan walked by. Cameron and Dylan were two of their close guy friends. But it was pretty obvious to everyone that Cameron and Cloe secretly crushed on each other.

17

"What's everyone so excited about?" asked Cameron.

"Oh, you guys got here just in time," said Sasha. "Ysabel Florente is throwing a fashion show, and we need your help setting everything up."

"I don't know who Ysabel Florente is," said Cameron. "But I'm happy to help."

The girls were totally shocked. They knew Cameron didn't share their passion for fashion, but still . . . Not to recognize the name of the most famous designer? That just seemed crazy to them.

Dylan seemed just as surprised as the girls, though. "Ysabel Florente is huge, dude. Who do you think designed the shoes I'm wearing?"

"Uh, honestly, it never occurred to me to think about it," said Cameron. "So what can I do?"

"You can help build the runway," said Sasha, checking that task off her list.

"Cool deal," said Cameron.

"Hey, what about me?" asked Dylan. "I want to hang backstage. VIP all the way, baby."

"We're not there to hang," Sasha reminded him. "We're there to work."

"Fine," said Dylan. "Sign me up to work."

Sasha checked her list and said, "You can work with the lighting people."

"Okay," said Dylan. "I'm totally down with that."

"Hey, Cloe," said Cameron. "What are *you* doing to help with the fashion show?"

"I'm not sure," she said, looking at Sasha.

Cameron thought for a second. "You know, with your excellent artistic talent you should really help out with the stage."

Cloe said, "Sure, that sounds great. Sign me up. Good idea, Cameron."

Everyone except Cloe and Cameron giggled.

"What's so funny?" Cameron asked.

"Got me," said Cloe with a shrug.

The others didn't say anything. But everyone was thinking the same exact thing: Cameron always came up with excuses to be by Cloe's side.

Chapter 3

The next day was Wednesday or—as the girls saw it—the day they would meet Ysabel Florente and company.

After school, everyone went their separate ways. Around five-thirty, Cloe cruised around in her car, picking up her friends.

"Jade, I just love that top," said Cloe as Jade hopped into the front seat of the car.

Jade looked down at her gauzy black peasant blouse. She was wearing a gold tank top underneath. And, of course, she was in her dark blue Ysabel Florente capris.

"Thanks, Cloe. You're not lookin' so bad yourself."

Cloe was definitely more casual—in faded jeans, a blue hoodie, and a red baby-doll T-shirt with a yellow star on the front. She still looked stylin', though, especially with her platform mules. "Thanks, Kool Kat," she said.

"Anytime, Angel," Jade replied. Angel was Cloe's nickname.

They picked up Sasha next. She was all business in her black suit. But it was still fabulous. The jacket had a big silver buckle and the pants were tight with flared bottoms. Plus, she was wearing a super-cute camisole underneath. It was red with shiny silver circles painted on it.

Next they arrived at Yasmin's, but she

wasn't quite ready.

"This is so weird," said Cloe after they'd spent five minutes waiting in front of Yasmin's house.

"I know," Jade agreed. "Yasmin is never late. That would be so inconsiderate and Yasmin is never inconsiderate."

"I wonder what's up," Sasha chimed in as she frowned down at her watch. "She's more excited than any of us about this."

A whole fifteen minutes went by before Yasmin came running out to the car, totally breathless. "Sorry," she told her friends, opening the door and climbing into the backseat. "Everyone looks so tricked out and fabulous and I'm a wreck."

"Not true," said Jade. "But what happened to your hair?"

It was a fashion disaster. Yasmin's hair was all plastered to one side. She looked as if she was close to tears. "I was trying out this new gel and I went overboard. I just wanted to make a good impression for Ysabel. Now she's going to think I'm a mess."

"Don't worry about it, babe. We'll make it all better," Sasha promised. "Cloe, tools please."

Cloe opened up her glove compartment and pulled out two brushes—one round and one regular.

Jade dug around in her purse until she found a hair clip with pretty blue gemstones. She handed it over to Sasha, who got to work on Yasmin's hair.

By the time Cloe pulled into the driveway at school, all the sticky gel had been brushed out, and Yasmin's hair was silky smooth. She was back to her regular look: gorgeous.

After Cloe parked, the Bratz climbed out of the car and checked their outfits for wrinkles.

"This is gonna be so cool," Jade exclaimed.

As the girls strolled through the parking lot toward the gymnasium entrance, they couldn't believe their eyes. There were vans and trucks and sound and lighting equipment everywhere.

"I knew the show was supposed to be big, but this is unbelievable," Cloe said.

"*Hello,*" said Jade. "Ysabel is the coolest of the cool. I wouldn't expect anything less."

"Check that out," said Sasha. She pointed

to a sleek-looking car with a custom paint job. It was white with green and red racing stripes.

"Wow," said Cloe. "That car is off the hook! I wonder whose it is."

Yasmin piped up. "It's Ysabel's," she said. "White, green, and red are the colors of the Italian flag. It's a hybrid, too. You know that's way better for the environment than a regular car. Ysabel bought it a couple of years ago. It was a present she gave herself after opening up her first store in Beverly Hills."

"Cool," said Sasha.

"Fabulous," Jade added.

"I totally have butterflies in my stomach right now," said Yasmin. "Is my hair okay?"

"You look great," said Cloe, trying to

reassure Yasmin. She could tell that she was more excited than usual.

Just then, Yasmin saw someone heading to the back door. She was dressed in casual Ysabel Florente jeans and a baby-blue tank top with bright pink trim. On her feet, she was sporting funky, chunky, high-heel boots. She was also wearing large, dark shades and a newsboy cap pulled down low.

Yasmin left the group and hustled over to the woman. As she got closer, she realized it was just whom she'd thought—Ysabel Florente.

Yasmin gave Ysabel her brightest smile. "Hi, I'm Yasmin, but call me Pretty Princess. All my friends do. I'm gonna be your personal assistant for the show. So anything you need, just ask, okay? I love your clothes and I love what you're doing for the environment. I'm a vegetarian, too. Oh, and your car is so totally rockin'. I've seen pictures, but they've got nothing on the real thing. Did you really import it from Switzerland?"

Yasmin continued to babble on with excitement. She didn't even notice that Ysabel was standing there, unenthused.

Finally Ysabel held up her hand. "Whoa there, Yasmin, slow down. You say you're my assistant for the next few days?"

"Yup." Yasmin smiled even more brightly. "Anything you need, just ask, okay?"

"Okay, first thing I need is some privacy," Ysabel replied, and without another word, she walked through the door and slammed it in Yasmin's face.

Yasmin stood there, staring at the closed door. *Did this really happen?* she wondered. *Was I really just dissed by my idol?*

Chapter 4

Shocked, crushed, and on the verge of tears, Yasmin went running back to her friends.

"I can't believe she did that," said Cloe. "What a snob!"

"I don't care how cutting-edge her fashions are," said Jade. "No one treats my friend that way."

Yasmin sniffed. "No, it's my fault. I bombarded her. I shouldn't have been so, so I don't know."

"You were excited," said Sasha. "Nothin' wrong with that."

"She's the one with the problem," Jade agreed.

"Let's just forget about it," said Yasmin. "I'm fine, really." She didn't sound fine though.

"We don't have to go through with this," said Cloe. "We can bail. That was so uncool."

"No," said Yasmin. "We signed up to do a good job and that's why we're here. So come on. Let's go in."

They headed for the gym. Once inside, they couldn't believe their eyes. The room was stylin'. It was as if they'd walked into some cool music video.

The gym had been totally transformed. Each wall was painted a different color. One red, one yellow, one green, and one blue. There were disco balls hanging from the ceiling, giving the whole place a retro look. And the old wooden, scratched floor was replaced with alternating black-and-white tile. There was also a DJ station in one corner. And the bleachers were carpeted in lush, red velvet.

"How utterly fabulous," said a breathless Jade. "They've obviously got some major talent on staff."

"Think we could get them to leave it like this after the show?" Cloe wondered.

"Don't I wish," said Sasha.

Ysabel's crew was hard at work, putting the runway together. Cameron had beaten the girls to the set and he was already working with the group.

The girls were on their way over to say hi when someone approached. He was a tall guy with a very large stomach poking out from his way-too-tight shirt. He had a funny-looking, thick beard. His pants were *way* too short, and he wore a long, bulky brown coat. "Who are you?" he asked them. "I don't remember clearing you to come in."

"Hello, sir," said Cloe. "We go to Stiles High and we're volunteering to help Ysabel Florente set up the show."

"I don't know about this," said the man.

"Who are you?" wondered Sasha.

"I'm Jack, the head of security," he answered. "Now you have to answer some questions. Please tell me your names and what you are doing here."

The girls were shocked. This guy in the polyester pants was giving them the third degree. What was up with that?

Sasha stepped forward and said, "Like my friend just said, we're the student volunteers. I'm Sasha. This is Jade, Cloe, and Yasmin. We've got a passion for fashion and we're ready to help make this show the best this town has ever seen."

"Okay, whatever," grumbled Jack. "Just stay out of my way." Turning around, he stormed off in a huff.

"What's his problem?" wondered Yasmin.

"Ooh, ooh, ooh!" Jade exclaimed, pointing toward one corner of the room. A wall was set up and it had a sign on it that said *Dressing Room*. "I'll bet the models are all in there."

Without giving polyester-pants dude another thought, the girls ran to the dressing room and knocked on the door.

"Hi, I'm Zank," said the tall model who answered the door. He had dark curly hair and mocha-colored skin. He had the brightest smile and very nice, big brown eyes. In short, he was a total cutie.

"I'm Sasha and these are my friends, Yasmin, Jade, and Cloe. We go to Stiles High and we've volunteered to help everyone get ready for the show," said Sasha.

"That's awesome," said Zank. "Come on in. We could definitely use the help."

The girls could hardly believe they were in a real models' dressing room. Looking around, they saw racks and racks of cool clothes. There was one giant full-length mirror and three desks. Each had a small mirror and a make-up station.

"I'm a big fan of your work," Jade said to Zank. "I saw you on the cover of *Runway Sensation* last month. And you had that awesome spread in *Fashion Forward* the month before that."

Zank smiled. "Thanks, but it wasn't a big deal. Come meet Chaz."

One of the other models walked over to them. He wasn't as tall as Zank, but he was just as cute. He had dark blond hair, sky-high cheekbones, and a mischievous smile.

"Hey," was all he said. His voice was soft, and he was blushing. He seemed just as sweet as Zank but way more shy.

Just then a very tall woman breezed by.

"Emma, come meet our volunteers," said Zank. "These girls are going to help us get ready for the big night."

"Hey there," said Emma, flashing everyone a warm smile. She had long, silky dark hair and eyes that were bright blue-green, like a tropical sea. "So nice to meet you."

"It's great to meet you," said Jade.

"Well, we don't want to get in your way," said Cloe. "The security guard has already given us a hard time. We'll just get to work now."

"Oh, don't pay any attention to him," said Zank. "He's way too uptight."

"No kidding," Emma said. "We tried complaining to Ysabel, but she won't listen to us.

She's so busy working on the show. I don't even think she's met the guy."

"She hasn't. Someone on the crew hired him," said Zank. "Anyway, you guys should just ignore Jake."

"Okay, I won't complain about that," Yasmin said. "But I thought his name was Jack."

Zank shrugged. "I'm pretty sure he told me it was Jake."

The girls left the dressing room.

Jade found the wardrobe people at the other end of the gym and went over to introduce herself.

Everyone else went to their stations, too—except for Yasmin, that is. She was left standing there. She just knew that Ysabel didn't like her, and guessed the designer was already on the phone, demanding a replacement assistant.

After sulking for a few minutes, she went to see Sasha, who was checking the MC's microphone. Sasha was fully in her element. She was cracking jokes with the sound people, and they all seemed to like her.

Just as Yasmin was about to say hello and introduce herself to everyone else, there was a huge crash followed by a scream. It came from the back of the gym.

Everyone ran toward the noise.

One of the spotlights had come crashing

down. The light had shattered and left a huge crack in the floor.

Cloe, Jade, Sasha, and Yasmin shuddered. They were all thinking the same thing—had someone been standing there, it would have been ugly.

"I can't believe it just broke like that," said Ysabel. "I wonder if the other lighting cords are worn out, too."

Yasmin bent down toward the light and picked up the cord. Studying it closely, she realized something strange. "This cord is brand-new. It's not worn out at all. There are no frayed edges and the break is totally clean. It looks like someone cut it on purpose."

But who?

Chapter 5

"Who would do something like that?" asked Cameron.

Cloe shrugged. "No idea." She looked from Jade to Yasmin to Dylan to Sasha.

No one had any guesses.

Ysabel stepped forward. "Everyone, please don't let this trip you up. We've got a show to put on and lots to finish before the curtain rises." With that, the designer stormed back into her office.

Everyone got back to work, except for Yasmin. Not knowing what to do with herself, she sat down by the coffee station and munched on some soy nuts.

Soon she saw a familiar-looking woman lurking around the corner. She was dressed in all black and she had white-blond hair and large, pale blue eyes. Curious, Yasmin went over to see who it was. The woman had opened up one of Ysabel's portfolios and was snapping pictures of her new designs.

Yasmin gasped. She suddenly realized why the woman looked so familiar. She was Sophia Noche, *another* famous designer. Yasmin wasn't crazy about Sophia Noche's line. Her clothes were kind of drab. She designed lots of stuff in colors like steel gray, honey, and wheat. Still, Yasmin had to respect her. Sophia had built a huge business all by herself. But why was she taking pictures of Ysabel's designs? Maybe ... so she could copy them? Would she do something so low?

Yasmin had to do something. "Can I help you?" she asked, tapping Sophia on the shoulder.

Sophia jumped back. Her face turned bright red. "No, no not at all. I'm fine. I was just..."

"Aren't you Sophia Noche?" asked Yasmin.

"Who wants to know?" asked Sophia, crossing her arms over her chest and glaring at Yasmin.

"Well, I do, for one," said Yasmin. "And I'm sure Ysabel would like to know you're here taking pictures of her designs."

"Are you calling me a thief?" asked Sophia angrily.

"No," said Yasmin. "I was just wondering ..."

"You know, Ysabel is the thief. She's the one who stole Zank right out from under my nose. He was my top model."

"Stole Zank?" asked Yasmin. "I don't know what you're talking about."

Just then Cloe walked by. "Hey, girl, what's up?" she asked.

"Great," said Yasmin, totally relieved that her friend showed up. "Sophia, meet Cloe. Cloe, meet Sophia Noche."

"*The* Sophia Noche?" asked Cloe.

"Yup," said Yasmin.

"I really need to get out of here," said Sophia,

starting to back away.

"Wait!" said Yasmin. "You can't leave yet. Cloe is a huge fan. She has a ton of questions for you." Leaning in close to Cloe, Yasmin whispered, "Don't let her leave, okay? I'll be right back."

Once she saw that Cloe got her message, Yasmin ran over to the models' dressing room and knocked on the door frantically. "Zank, are you there?" she shouted. "Zank, come out."

Zank answered the door and said, "What's up?"

"Follow me," said Yasmin, grabbing his hand. She explained the situation as she brought him over to Sophia, who was now trying to get away from Cloe.

Zank went right up to Sophia. "Hey, what

are you doing here?" he asked.

"Just coming to see what Ysabel stole from me," said Sophia.

Zank tried to explain. "Look, Sophia, I'm sorry about what happened, but you can't blame Ysabel. My contract with you was up and it was time for me to try something new."

"You want new? You should see my spring line," said Sophia. "Totally cutting-edge. It was a huge hit in Paris. We're due in Milan in two weeks. We really need you, Zank. You have to come back to us."

"Sorry," said Zank. "I'm happy modeling Ysabel's clothes. Plus, a percentage of her proceeds goes to charity."

Sophia narrowed her eyes at Zank. "You're

gonna regret this," she grumbled. Turning to the small group that had gathered to watch her major meltdown, she shouted, "All of you will!" Then she stalked off, slamming the gymnasium door shut behind her.

Chapter 6

Sophia made so much noise that everyone came over to see what was going on. But before anyone could even ask any questions, Emma ran over in a total panic. "Ysabel, I have horrible news," she said. "Someone has stained your entire new line of clothing. Everything that's supposed to be modeled on Saturday night is ruined."

"Yeah. Someone named Sophia," Yasmin whispered to herself.

Ysabel's jaw dropped. "We can't go on. It's all over," she cried. "I'm cancelling the show."

"Wait a minute," said Yasmin. "We can fix the clothes. All we need is a bottle of Nifty Jifty Stain Remover."

"Oh come on," said Ysabel. "Do you really think that'll work?" From the tone of her voice, it was obvious that she didn't.

"Totally," said Yasmin, staying positive. "It's the best, especially when you mix it with seltzer and baking soda."

"Well, do you have any?" asked Ysabel.

"No," said Yasmin. "But I can get it. All I need is a ride to the drugstore and about half an hour. This is a fashion disaster that I can handle, no prob."

"We've got nothing else to lose," said Ysabel with a shrug. "I doubt it'll work, but I'm getting desperate here."

Once Yasmin got what she needed, she and her friends gathered in the models' dressing room with all of the stained clothing.

"It's totally criminal to harm something as beautiful as this," said Sasha. She was holding up a funky denim mini-dress. "I mean it—whoever did this should be thrown in jail."

"Whoever did this has some serious issues with Ysabel," said Cloe. "Do you think it was Sophia Noche?"

"Probably," said Sasha. "I can't believe she got in here. I mean, I thought there was security around this place. We got stopped."

Yasmin waved a hairdryer over some of the already clean but still wet clothing. She acted carefully, so as not to burn any holes with the hot air. "I think we need to figure out who's behind all this mischief and mayhem. You could be right about Sophia, but we should make sure. I mean, come on. We can't let the show fail."

Cloe, Sasha, and Jade agreed. If only they knew what to do . . .

Chapter 7

The next day on the set, things were even worse. The new runway had been destroyed after someone sawed off all its legs.

And that was just the beginning.

An hour later, Chaz was pacing back and forth, acting like a total spaz. "My new shampoo? Gone. Totally gone," he said. "How am I supposed to go onstage if I can't wash my hair? There's no replacing that shampoo. It's imported from Italy."

"The make-up is missing," said Emma, racing into the room. "There was a brand-new shipment stacked up under the bleachers, and now it's gone."

"Whose make-up was it?" Sasha wondered.

"Everybody's make-up," Emma replied.

Suddenly there was another scream. Loud and intense, it was coming from Ysabel's dressing room. She emerged a few moments later, looking as pale white as a ghost.

"What happened now?" asked Cloe.

Ysabel handed her a small brown bag. "I ordered dinner from the local vegetarian café. It

56

was supposed to be mushroom barley tofu stew. But they sent me this instead."

Yasmin looked inside. She saw large pieces of beef floating around in a soupy mixture. "Beef stew."

"And that's not all," said Ysabel, handing Cloe a note. "I found this taped to the lid."

The note read: *You've already been warned. Now cancel the show, or else . . .*

"This is awful," said Cloe. "We have to do something."

Ysabel glared at Cloe, Jade, Yasmin, and Sasha. "Do something? You four? Why, everything was fine until you showed up. I think you've all done enough!"

Chapter 8

Ysabel canceled rehearsal for the rest of the night.

Everyone was so upset, they hardly spoke the entire drive home. But the next day at lunch they met up to discuss the situation.

"Okay," said Sasha, once they'd all settled in their seats. "It's obvious that someone doesn't want Ysabel Florente to have her show at Stiles High. But who? And why?"

Sasha took a sip of her berry blast smoothie before she spoke. "I don't know, but we have to save the fashion show. Plus, right now I have the feeling that Ysabel blames us. We can't just let that slide."

"Too true," Cloe piped in, before taking a bite of her sandwich.

"Maybe it's Sophia Noche," said Yasmin. "She's really mad that Zank works for Ysabel now, and she was taking pictures of Ysabel's designs."

"Could be," said Jade. But we've got to be sure, before we can accuse her of anything.

"So what do we do?" asked Cloe. Because we've got to make sure this fashion show happens."

"There's only one person who can help us," said Sasha. "Ysabel Florente. Yasmin, you're going to have to talk to her."

Yasmin pouted and slammed her strawberry

mango smoothie down on the table. "No way. Ysabel can't stand me," she cried. "She thinks I'm a total pest."

"But what about the animals?" pleaded Jade.

Chapter 9

That night, Yasmin decided to swallow her pride. She took a deep breath and knocked on Ysabel's dressing room door.

"Who is it?" asked Ysabel.

After the way Ysabel had been treating her, Yasmin felt very nervous around the designer. "If this is a bad time, I can come back later. But I really need to talk to you."

Ysabel opened up the door. "What do you want?"

No turning back now, thought Yasmin. She marched into the dressing room. "Look," she said, "all I've ever done is try and be nice to you. It's okay that you don't like me. I can deal. This isn't about me. My friends and I are going to figure out who's behind this mess because your fashion show has to go on. But I need your help."

"I don't know what you expect me to do," said Ysabel. "I'm a designer. I design clothes. I put on fashion shows. That's it. All this mischief out there—" She waved a hand, gesturing toward the set. "I don't get it."

"Well, if you talk to me, maybe my girls and I can figure it out," Yasmin insisted. "We think maybe Sophia Noche is to blame, but I need to know for sure. So tell me, is there anyone else with a grudge against you? Give me the 411, okay?"

"Wow," said Ysabel, looking rather shocked. "You really want to help me after I've been so rude?"

"Your fashions rock," said Yasmin. "Despite your attitude."

"I'm so sorry about that," said Ysabel. "I've been awful. There's no excuse. My problems have nothing to do with you."

"Could have fooled me," muttered Yasmin. She couldn't help it.

"Okay, I deserve that," said Ysabel. "Please sit down. I owe you an explanation." Ysabel pointed to the couch, and Yasmin sat down.

Ysabel sat across from her. "I'm sorry I snapped at you. Slamming the door in your face? It was horrible. And it isn't me at all. It's just been so stressful these days. This weird stuff started before we even got here. I've been getting threatening notes and prank calls for weeks. Last Saturday, someone even slashed the tires on my car."

"That stinks," said Yasmin. "Do you think Sophia Noche may be behind this?"

"Maybe," Ysabel replied. "Sophia is really competitive with me. On the other hand, she's not violent. I just can't see her pulling that lighting trick. Sophia wants to *hire* my models, not *injure* them."

"Well, then who could it be? Is there anyone else who might want to hurt you?" Yasmin wondered.

Ysabel closed her eyes. "I don't know."

Chapter 10

Yasmin left Ysabel to have a look around. There were people in every part of the gym. Sasha was in the sound booth with the drummer and guitar player who were going to perform live at the show. Dylan was helping the lighting people replace the fixture that had crashed. Cloe and Cameron were fixing the stage. And Jade was hanging out in the dressing room with the models. But there was no sign of Sophia.

Since she wasn't inside, Yasmin checked out the parking lot.

It looked empty, but as Yasmin crept

around the parked cars to head back, she heard a noise coming from a truck parked close to the gymnasium's entrance. It sounded like a series of snapping noises. She peeked inside to find the head of security. He had a large pile of shoes in front of him and he was snapping off their heels, one by one.

She hurried back inside the gym and headed straight for Ysabel's office.

"I think I found out what's going on," said Yasmin, once Ysabel let her in.

"Who is it?" asked Ysabel.

"That's what's so weird," said Yasmin. "Follow me quickly."

Yasmin led Ysabel to the truck, where Jack/ Jake was still wrecking shoes.

Ysabel gasped. "That's not the security guard," she whispered. "That's Paul, my ex-manager."

"Huh?" asked Yasmin.

Ysabel pulled Yasmin away from the truck. Once she was sure they were out of earshot, she explained. "We got into a huge fight last month. I had to fire him because he was pressuring me to make some designs for fur coats. I said no way, of course. So then he asked me to create a line of faux-fur stuff. That I have no problem with. But the thing is he switched manufacturers."

"What do you mean?" Yasmin asked.

Ysabel said, "He took my faux-fur designs to a place that works with real fur. He wasn't even going to tell me about it."

Yasmin gasped. "That's the worst!"

"I know," replied Ysabel. "Luckily I halted production just in time. And, of course, I fired Paul immediately. No one lies to me and gets away with it. Especially when the welfare of animals is involved." Ysabel looked worriedly toward the truck. "He said he'd get revenge. I didn't take him seriously at the time . . ."

"Creepy," said Yasmin.

"Can't argue with you there," Ysabel said. "So what's the plan?"

"Wait here," said Yasmin. "I'll be right back."

Yasmin headed back to the gym and made an announcement. "Attention, everyone. I've found the guy who's been trying to ruin the show."

"No way," said Cameron, the first to jump up.

"Who is it?" wondered Emma.

"If you could all just drop what you're doing and follow me outside," said Yasmin.

Yasmin, Cloe, Sasha, Jade, Cameron, Dylan, the crew, and the models all tiptoed outside to the truck.

Ysabel opened the door to reveal the head of security. "Paul!" she yelled, completely surprising him. "How could you?"

Rather than answer, Paul made a run for it.

Everyone chased him around the parking lot.

Yasmin came close to capturing him by Ysabel's car, but he managed to get away. Sasha

71

almost had him when he tripped over his own shoelace, but he darted around her at the last second.

He headed for the parking lot exit, but Zank, Cameron, Cloe, and some of the musicians made a human chain, blocking off the area just in time.

Paul was left with no choice but to run back inside the gym.

Luckily, the group was hot on his heels.

After a failed attempt to escape through a window—Paul was too large to fit through—he headed through the dressing room door.

Emma was the one who finally cornered him there. Slamming the door closed on his face, she locked him inside.

Then Yasmin called the cops, who came quickly to take Paul away.

* * *

"Thank you all so much," said Zank, once everything had been settled. He gave each of the girls hugs. "You saved the show."

"No time to celebrate now," said Ysabel. "We have a fashion show to put on."

"She's right," said Emma. "But how are we going to manage? We can't strut down the runway barefoot."

"You won't need to," said Yasmin, stepping forward. "Does anyone have any superglue?"

"Great idea, Pretty Princess," said Sasha. Turning to Ysabel she said, "We'll fix all the shoes in no time."

"You girls are amazing," said Ysabel. "Thank you for fixing everything." Shaking her head sadly, she added, "This is all my fault. I was so busy running the show that I never took the time to notice who was working security."

"Hey, no worries," said Yasmin. "Your fashions rock, and the show is going to be perfect!"

Chapter 11

The next day was Saturday. Fashion-show day!

Hip-hop music blared from the speakers. It was a surround-sound sensation. The Bratz all felt the music coming from a place deep within.

They swayed to the beat as Ysabel's models sashayed down the runway, waving their arms and swinging their hips. The show was amazing. Zank, Chaz, and Emma all looked fabulous. Ysabel had designed the most amazing clothes. They were totally killer, not to mention groundbreaking.

The audience went wild.

And the Bratz were watching from backstage. It was so fabulous. Each design was cooler and more cutting-edge than the one before it.

After Chaz made his last trip down the runway, Ysabel got up on stage and took a bow. The crowd went mad with applause.

Even through the microphone, Ysabel had to shout. "I'd like to thank Stiles High for hosting this event," she said. "Especially Cloe, Jade, Sasha, Cameron, and Dylan. You all did amazing work. And I'd like to thank you all for showing up to support me and the local animal shelter. Proceeds from this evening are going to be donated to that worthy cause."

Yasmin blinked back her tears. Did she hear

correctly? She'd thought that she and her favorite designer were finally on good terms. But Ysabel Florente didn't even mention her.

She wanted to run home and cry, but she was frozen with shock and sadness. She couldn't move at all.

Ysabel said, "I have a surprise for everyone. There's one more fashion. It's a new style of jeans that'll be modeled by Emma. I'm calling it Pretty Princess. That's what everyone calls my new friend, Yasmin. Tonight almost didn't happen. And we have Yasmin to thank for saving the show. So everyone, please give her a hand."

The music started up again. Emma walked down the runway in the most gorgeous jeans.

They were dark blue and perfectly worn in, with a cool fringe around the pockets and at the bottom. There were even cute sparkles running down the sides—purple on one side and pink on the other.

Yasmin was beaming. And her friends were, too. Just being close to Ysabel and behind the scenes was a dream-come-true. But having an entire style of jeans named after her? And having Ysabel call her a friend? There were no words to describe how that felt.

After the show, Yasmin, Cloe, Sasha, Jade, Dylan, and Cameron got to party backstage with the models and company.

Ysabel pushed through the anxious crowd of reporters and photographers. "Where's Pretty Princess?" she asked.

Yasmin turned around and said, "I'm right here. What's up?"

Ysabel gave her a hug and said, "Thank you so much. All of you girls are amazing. We seriously could not have done this without you."

Everyone got together for a group hug.

Then Dylan turned up the music, and everybody danced like crazy.

"The mural, I almost forgot," Jade shouted over the music to Yasmin. Would it be all right with you if I painted myself in Pretty Princess Jeans?"

"That would be fashion-tastic," Yasmin said, smiling.

Yasmin, Cloe, Jade, and Sasha have fun wherever they are, but being behind the scenes that Saturday night? Partying with Ysabel Florente after the hottest fashion show of the year? It was even more rockin' than usual.